MARIO'S MAYAN JOURNEY

MEXICO

Mexico
City

Gulf of

Pacific Ocean

Río
Lagartos

Celestún

Chichén Itzá
Ruins

Mexico

Bay of Campeche

Tulum
Ruins

YUCATÁN
PENINSULA

Palenque
Ruins

Yaxchilán
Ruins

Tikal
Ruins

BELIZE

*Caribbean
Sea*

GUATEMALA

HONDURAS

MARIO'S MAYAN JOURNEY

BY MICHELLE MCCUNNEY

To my father, Stanley

The illustrations in this book were done in watercolor on Arches paper.

For information contact:
MONDO Publishing
980 Avenue of the Americas
New York, NY 10018
Visit our web site at http://www.mondopub.com

Printed in Hong Kong by South China Printing Co. (1988) Ltd.
04 05 06 07 08   9 8 7 6 5

Designed by Edward Miller

Library of Congress Cataloging-in-Publication Data
McCunney, Michelle.
Mario's Mayan journey / Michelle McCunney [author and illustrator].
p.   cm.
Summary: A young Mexican dreams that he meets two Mayan children and together they visit the ancient ruins in the jungles of the Yucátan Peninsula.
ISBN 1-57255-204-2 (hc). — ISBN 1-57255-203-4 (pb)
[1. Mexico—Fiction.   2. Yucátan (Mexico : State)—Fiction.   3. Dreams—Fiction.
4. Mayas—Fiction.]   I. Title.
PZ7.M478415 Mar   1996
[Fic]—dc20   95-39407
CIP
AC

AUTHOR'S NOTE

Two things I have always enjoyed are dreaming about places I would like to visit, and actually visiting them. But dreaming about them is more than half the fun.

Before I visited the Yucatán Peninsula, in Mexico, I read about the ruins there and about ancient Mayan culture. When I visited the ruins at Chichén Itzá, Uxmal, Sayil, and Labná, it was exciting to see the things I had imagined in my dreams, like the red jaguar throne inside the pyramid at Chichén Itzá. It wouldn't have been so exciting to see it if I hadn't dreamed about it first.

I'm still dreaming about visiting the ancient cities of Yaxchilán and Tikal, and of someday wandering through a jungle and catching sight of a howler monkey.

Mario lived in Mexico City. His mother and father had moved
there from Southern Mexico before he was born.

Mario's parents often talked about the South and the Mayan people
who lived there. Sometimes his father described ancient Mayan ruins
he had seen in the jungles of the Yucatán Peninsula. Mario searched
for these places on the map and spent hours looking at clay figures,
stone sculptures, and ancient wall paintings in the Mayan Room of
the anthropology museum.

One night, Mario lay in his bed listening to the familiar sounds of the apartment building where he lived. He could hear the upstairs neighbor's footsteps and the downstairs neighbor's radio. An airplane flew overhead and cars on the avenue honked their horns. Mario held his breath and tried to hear the footsteps of an ocelot or the cry of a macaw.

"Caw!" Mario woke up with a start. He was in a hammock! It was morning and the birds outside called loudly. No one else was in the room, but there were some delicious-looking tortillas and a steaming bowl of black beans on a small table near his hammock. Mario ate breakfast quickly and went outside.

In the garden there were two children waiting for Mario. Their names were Fernando and Margarita. They spoke to Mario in Mayan at first, but they switched to Spanish when he didn't understand. "Ven con nosotros," they said. "Come with us."

With a basket of tortillas, a large piece of cheese, several mangoes, and a gourd full of water, they set off down the river in the direction of the sea.

The day was warm and still.

They reached a place where white pelicans waded and a rare quetzal flashed its blue-green feathers. *Tac-a-tac-a-tac.* A toucan snapped at the air hungrily as the travelers ate their lunch.

Then there was a different cry that was much louder than the others. *Yeeeooow!* It came from howler monkeys high in the branches. Mario shivered. He tried to catch a glimpse of one of the shrieking monkeys, but they were well hidden.

Flap, flap, flap! A flock of flamingos passed by overhead. "Acompáñenos a Chichén Itzá!" they cried. "Come with us to Chichén Itzá!"

Holding tightly to the flamingos' legs, Mario and his friends floated up and away from the river and over a sea of green treetops.

Soon they could see white stone pyramids rising above the trees below—the ancient Mayan city of Chichén Itzá!

The flamingos flew lower and dropped their charges gently on top of the Temple of Warriors.

Inside the temple there was a fascinating wall painting of an ancient Mayan village. As they stood looking, Mario wondered about the ancestors who had made the mural. They had also traveled in canoes, and maybe they had spoken the same Mayan language as Fernando and Margarita. Had they also spoken with flamingos and shivered at the sound of howler monkeys?

"Vamos a la selva!" said Fernando. "Let's go to the jungle!"

They walked out of the city and into the jungle beyond.

It was getting late. Mario helped Fernando and Margarita make a palm leaf shelter to sleep in. Soon it was too dark to see, and they settled down to sleep.

As night fell, the jungle was full of sounds. A macaw gave a loud screech, and a jaguar growled and sharpened its claws. Mario heard the peaceful sounds of sleep from Fernando and Margarita and closed his eyes.

In the morning, Mario realized he was in his room in the city. Downstairs someone was listening to the radio. Cars on the avenue were honking their horns.

Was it a dream? Mario thought for a moment and tried to remember everything—the sounds and colors, Margarita and Fernando, the excitement he had felt when he saw the flamingos and heard the howler monkeys.

Then Mario remembered the mural paintings he had seen in Chichén Itzá, and he had an idea. He would paint pictures of what he had seen so he would never forget any of it.

And that is what he did.

GLOSSARY

anthropology (an-thruh-POL-uh-gee) the science that studies the beginning, development, behavior, and customs of human beings

Chichén Itzá (chee-CHEN eet-SAH) an ancient Mayan city of central Yucatán in Mexico

gourd (goord) a fruit with a hard rind that can be used as a container when dried

howler monkey (HOW-ler MUN-key) a type of monkey with a long tail and an extremely loud, howling call

jaguar (JAG-wahr) a large wildcat of Central and South America with a yellowish coat and black spots

macaw (muh-KAW) a large, brightly-colored bird of Central and South America with a long tail, curved powerful bill, and harsh cry

mango (MAN-go) a sweet, juicy tropical fruit

Maya (MY-uh) a member of the Indian people of southeast Mexico, Guatemala, Belize, Honduras, and El Salvador; the Maya are noted for their architecture and city planning, their mathematics and calendar, and their writing system

ocelot (AHS-eh-lot) a wildcat with a grayish or yellowish coat and black spots

quetzal (ket-SAHL) a Central American bird with brilliant green and red feathers

tortilla (tor-TEE-ah) a thin disk of flat bread made from cornmeal or wheat flour and baked on a hot surface

toucan (TOO-kan) a tropical bird with bright feathers and a very large beak that curves downward

Yucatán Peninsula (yoo-ka-TAN pe-NIN-suh-la) a piece of land mostly in southeast Mexico that juts out between the Caribbean Sea and the Gulf of Mexico

MEXICO

Gulf of

Mexico
City

Pacific Ocean

Mexico

Celestún

Río
Lagartos

Chichén Itzá
Ruins

Tulum
Ruins

Bay of Campeche

YUCATÁN
PENINSULA

Palenque
Ruins

Yaxchilán
Ruins

Tikal
Ruins

BELIZE

Caribbean
Sea

GUATEMALA

HONDURAS